ANDY PANDY'S
annual

Illustrated by Phil Gascoigne

PURNELL
London

75p.

ANDY PANDY'S NEW ROMPERS

One morning Andy caught his rompers on a nail in the garden shed and tore a big hole in them. Teddy was very sorry for him but Andy said it didn't matter because he needed some new ones and would begin to make some that very day.

"And this time I shall make some pockets in them," he said.

"I wish I could have some pockets," Teddy said.

"But you don't wear clothes," said Andy. "You don't need to because you are covered with nice soft warm fur."

"All the same," said Teddy, "I should like some pockets." He followed Andy upstairs to the cupboard where there was a big roll of blue and white striped cotton. He pulled it out and then found a paper pattern and some scissors and went downstairs. But first he took off his torn rompers and put on his best ones.

"May I help you make some new rompers?" Teddy asked as he watched Andy spread the material flat on the floor and unfold the paper pattern.

"If you could fetch the pin-box and give me the pins one by one that would be a great help."

Teddy trotted off and came back with the pin box but picking up pins one at a time with fat furry paws isn't as easy as picking them up with fingers and he dropped so many that he began to cry.

"I'm not helping at all," he said, and he looked so sad that Andy had to think of a way to make him happy again.

"Stop crying, Teddy," he said, "and I'll make you two pockets to tie round your waist out of my old rompers." Teddy was all smiles in two seconds. "I *can* help with them, can't I, Andy?" he said running to fetch his own pair of scissors. They have round ends so that he can't hurt himself if he falls over while he is holding them.

While he was looking for them (for Teddy's things are *never* where they ought to be) Andy Pandy pinned the paper pattern on to the blue and white striped cotton ready to be cut out. When Teddy came back he gave him the old rompers and said, "Cut along all the seams, Teddy, and then we'll spread it all out on the floor and cut out your pockets from the best pieces." Teddy was very happy. The two things he likes doing most of all are cutting up things and playing with water.

For a while all was quiet, with Andy carefully cutting round the paper pattern for his new rompers and Teddy slashing away at the old ones. At last they were both ready to begin sewing but at that very moment in rushed Rags and the White Kitten. Andy

just managed to get his work off the floor and on to the table but Teddy wasn't quite quick enough and Rags pounced upon his and raced off with it with the White Kitten after him. "Oh dear," cried Teddy, "Now my work will be all spoilt." "No, it won't," Andy said. "Run after them and get it back. We'll have to wash it anyway so it won't matter if they've made it dirty." Teddy ran out into the garden and there were those naughty animals pulling

and tugging at the stuff trying to tear it in half. They dropped it when they saw Teddy coming, and went and hid under the bushes while he went indoors and smoothed out the crumples.

Andy helped him and then said, "Now first we must make two little bags."

"Big ones," said Teddy.

"Well, big enough," Andy said. "Then we must sew them on to a sort of belt to tie round your waist and there will be two pockets."

"Must I have a paper pattern?" Teddy asked.

"Yes," Andy said. "I'll cut you one out of a piece of brown paper." He cut an oblong piece and showed Teddy how when it was folded in half it

could be made into a bag and then he pinned it on to one of the best parts of the old rompers and said they would cut out the second pocket when they had done the first. He wanted to get on with his own sewing so he left Teddy to himself. Neither of them saw Rags and the White Kitten looking at them through the window.

"It isn't fair," growled Rags. "If they can play with bits of stuff why can't we?"

"And now they've got some reels of cotton," said the White Kitten, "and if there's one thing I like more than another it's a reel of cotton to play with. Let's go in anyway."

Now although kittens can make no noise when they walk, dogs make a clatter because they don't draw in their claws as kittens do, so Teddy heard them coming and he scrambled up on to the table with his sewing so that they couldn't reach him. But the work basket was still on the floor and in no time at all, the White Kitten had a cotton reel in his mouth and was off like a shot. Rags had only time to snatch a tape measure before both Andy and Teddy were after them leaving

their work safe on the table.

When they had gone Looby Loo climbed up on to a chair and looked at Teddy's pockets. Andy had been too busy to look at them after they were cut out and they looked dreadful. All the edges which should have been straight were jagged and rough and Looby smiled as she picked up the scissors and began to straighten them. She had just managed to finish when she heard Andy and Teddy coming. So she slipped back into her corner and sat there looking as if she had never moved.

They had found the cotton reel but not the tape measure. As they settled down again Andy thought he had better see that Teddy's cutting out was all right and was surprised to see how beautifully straight the edges were. "You *have* done this nicely," he said.

"Yes, haven't I?" said Teddy who hadn't noticed the difference between Looby Loo's nice smooth edges and his jaggedy ones.

Andy folded the pockets and pinned them and showed Teddy where to sew them and then went back to his own work. They pinned and stitched and stitched and pinned and were as quiet as mice except that Andy always had to thread needles for Teddy and he needed a great many because somehow he always got knots in his cotton and had to start again.

Andy Pandy has a little sewing machine. It is only a toy but it sews very well and is much quicker than sewing long seams by hand. He offered to machine Teddy's pockets but Teddy said "No, thank you, Andy. I want to make my own pockets my own self."

So Andy turned the handle of the machine as fast as he could go and soon his piece of material began to look like a splendid pair of new rompers.

Teddy sewed away and then said "Shall I cut out the belt to go round my waist?"

"We'll have to measure you," Andy said, then he added, "but wait a minute, we'll have to go out and find the tape measure first." So once more they went out into the garden and looked everywhere for the tape measure and Rags and the White Kitten hid under the bushes and laughed at them, and once more Looby Loo got

up and looked at their work and did a bit of machining on Andy's and pulled out some of Teddy's huge uneven stitches and did them again. And once more when they came back after they had found the tape measure in the wood shed, she was sitting quietly in her corner looking as if she had never moved.

"Let's have tea before we go on with our sewing," Andy said. Teddy is always ready for tea and they spent a happy half hour in the kitchen eating honey and buns and drinking milk—they call it tea because they have it at tea time but they only drink milk and lemonade. Then, when they had finished, they went back to their needlework. "We'll clear the table after," Andy said.

Andy measured round Teddy's waist which is rather fat and then he cut out a long strip for the belt. "Let me just machine this bit, because it's rather long and we'll have a lot to do if we want to finish before we go to bed."

Teddy agreed. He was beginning to get a little tired of sewing so he was glad to be helped. He went on with his pockets and Andy finished the belt and went on with the new rompers. But then in came those two animals again. This time they went into the kitchen and helped themselves to buns and milk. It was easy for Rags to take the buns in his mouth but the White Kitten walked round the milk jug on the table and mewed.

"I can't get my head in the jug," he said, "and I'm thirsty."

"That's easy," said Rags and he put his paw on the jug and knocked it over. "Get down on the floor, there's a puddle of milk there already."

The White Kitten jumped down and began to lap, its little pink tongue popping in and out very fast. Then Rags thought he would do the same with the honey pot but instead of just tipping over, it crashed to the floor.

Of course Andy and Teddy heard it and rushed into the kitchen to see what was the matter. Rags and the White Kitten fled and weren't seen at all until it was bedtime. All the spilt milk and the honey had to be cleaned up and the pieces of broken honey pot thrown away and by the time all that was done they were both quite tired.

But Andy said, "I'm not going to bed until I've finished my new striped rompers."

Teddy was delighted at the thought of sitting up late so he said, "And I'm not going to bed until I've finished my new pockets." So they stitched and stitched and yawned and yawned and their eyes kept closing but they somehow stayed awake until the rompers were finished and the pockets were sewn on the belt.

"There," said Andy Pandy. "Let's take them upstairs and we can put them on first thing in the morning."

"I want to try mine on now," Teddy began but he was so tired that he fell asleep half way up the stairs and Andy had to carry him the rest of the way.

They both slept like logs and didn't move until the sun woke them shining through the window the next morning.

Teddy was up first. When

Andy sat up, still rubbing his eyes, he was busy fastening the belt with the two pockets, one hanging over each leg, looking very smart. But something was wrong with them. "Andy," he cried, "What's the matter with my pockets? I can't get my paws in them."

"Let me see." Andy went over to Teddy and then burst out laughing. "You silly little bear," he said. "You have sewn up the tops of the pockets so of course you can't get your paws in."

Teddy looked so disappointed that Andy Pandy said: "I expect it was because you were so tired. Never mind, we'll soon unstitch them."

"I do hope your rompers are all right," Teddy said.

"So do I," Andy said. "Wait a minute. I'll just go into the bathroom and wash and then I'll come back in them."

He went away and after a time Teddy heard him laughing. "Teddy," he called, "come and look."

Teddy went into the bathroom, then he too began to laugh. Andy's hands were hidden inside the sleeves and his feet were hidden inside the legs because he had sewn up the ends of the sleeves and the legs. He and Teddy had been so tired that they had just gone on stitching without knowing what they were doing.

"Who's a silly little bear now?" shouted Teddy, dancing about so that his pockets flapped up and down.

After breakfast they unpicked the sleeves and the legs and the tops of the pockets and Andy wore his new rompers and Teddy walked about with his paws in his pockets all day.

BIRDS

"What are those?" said Teddy
Pointing to the sky.
"All those little black things
Flying up so high?"

"They are birds," said Andy,
"Come from far away.
That means summer's coming
So they've come to stay."

Just then a tiny little bird
Flying round and round
Came tumbling through the
        sunny air
And fell down on the ground.

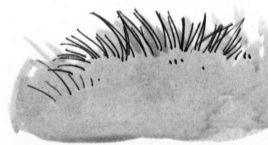

"The little bird is tired,
I think he needs a rest.
We'll take him home," said Andy,
"And make a tiny nest."

They put him in a shoe box
And gave him crumbs of bread
And water in a saucer.
Then he went to bed.

When the bird had rested
He chirped as if to say
"Thank you, Andy Pandy,"
And then he flew away.

MAKE A PUZZLE

You will need some plain postcards,
scissors and some paints

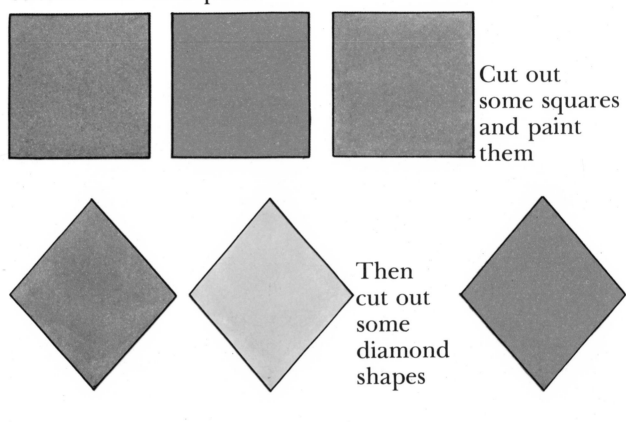

Cut out
some squares
and paint
them

Then
cut out
some
diamond
shapes

Cut some of the diamonds
into two pieces

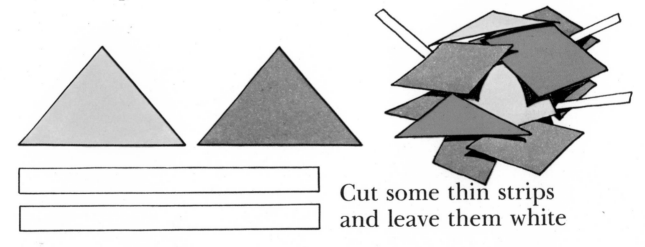

Cut some thin strips
and leave them white

MAKE UP DIFFERENT PATTERNS

WHICH GOOSE IS DIFFERENT?

LOOBY LOO AND THE LITTLE FAWN

Nearly every summer when the days are long and hot and sunny Teddy makes a fuss about going to bed. "It's still daytime," he says, "and who wants to go to bed in the daytime—only babies do that."

But sometimes Andy Pandy says that he can stay up as long as he likes and in no time at all, there he is yawning and hardly able to keep his eyes open and Andy almost has to carry him upstairs.

One evening, after the usual grumbles, Teddy and Andy Pandy went to bed and, because they had both been out of doors playing in the sun all day, they fell asleep as soon as their heads touched the pillow. Looby Loo waited until she was sure they were sound asleep before she sat up and then got very quietly out of her own bed and crept downstairs and crawled through the cat flap in the door.

In the kitchen, Rags and the White Kitten were nowhere to be seen although that is where their sleeping baskets are; they

too thought it was too early to go to bed. Looby was glad that they were not there because she didn't want them to follow her.

She meant to go a long way into the woods to see what it was like to be right in the middle of hundreds and hundreds of trees. The sun was shining through the leaves and as she ran down a little path, it

was covered with speckly light like golden coins. She was very happy.

Further and further she went singing to herself and stopping every now and then to listen to the birds. She saw a field mouse creep out from behind a big stone and a squirrel leap through the air from the branch of one tree to another. Then she heard a noise as if a much bigger animal was walking towards her and hiding herself she peeped through a hole in some bushes to see what it was.

He was a little fawn, a very young one. He was very pretty and had some light coloured spots on the back of its shining brown coat just like the spots of sunshine Looby had seen on the woodland path. She watched the fawn who seemed to be trying to stand up but its four long legs wouldn't go the way he wanted them to. They got themselves crossed or they slid slowly outwards and each time the fawn found himself back on the ground it looked so surprised that at last Looby Loo couldn't help laughing.

The fawn started back but she called out "Don't go away, little fawn, I won't hurt you. Perhaps I can help you to stand up." She came out from behind the bush and the fawn watched her with its big soft brown eyes. She held out her hand and as he didn't try to get up she knelt down beside him and put her arms round his neck. "It must be very young," she thought, "if it can't even

stand." He was, in fact, very young indeed, hardly a day old.

Looby stroked him and kissed the soft fur and said, "Can you talk?" "I don't know," said the fawn, "I've never tried." Looby laughed and said, "But you *are* talking," and the fawn was so pleased that he laughed too.

Then Looby Loo said, "Look, I will get down on all fours and pretend I have four legs like you and then you do what I do and you'll soon learn to stand."

The fawn watched her as she tried to make herself look as if she had four legs tucked under her just as he had. Then she lifted herself on her elbows and the fawn raised himself on his knees, then Looby put

her hands flat on the ground and tried to make her arms stiff like legs but they spread out flat and down she fell. The fawn did the same and they both lay face to face laughing.

Then Looby tried by making her arms and legs stiff and the fawn tried and tried but his long legs always slid away from him. At last Looby stood up and when the fawn managed to get all four feet on the ground at once she held him up. She still held him with her arms round his neck and together they walked a few steps. Suddenly they heard something behind them and a big deer came crashing through the trees.

She went at once to the little fawn and said, "Where have you been? I thought you were just behind me."

The fawn was so pleased to see his mother that he began to jump about and he didn't fall over once. "Look," he cried, "I'm walking, I'm standing, I'm not falling down."

"So you should be," said the big deer, "You're nearly a whole day old. Who is this?" she went on, turning her beautiful eyes towards Looby Loo.

"I don't know who she is but she is very kind and helped me to walk when my legs got in a muddle."

The mother deer said, "What is your name, little girl?"

"Looby Loo."

"Would you like to come and see where we live?"

"Oh yes, please," said Looby.

The deer went slowly away through the wood with Looby and the little fawn following. He chattered all the way. "Isn't everything pretty—doesn't it all smell lovely—what are those things called?"

"Flowers," said Looby.

"I'm so glad I'm me," said the fawn and he began to jump about again and bang went all his legs flat on the ground. Looby helped him up and whispered, "Don't talk so much, think about walking."

After a time they came to a wide grassy space between the trees and the mother deer said, "This is our home."

"It's like a house," Looby said. "With the walls made of trees and the roof of green leaves with the sun shining through—and the spaces between the trees are like windows and the grass makes a beautiful carpet."

"I don't know what a house is," said the deer, "but I am glad you like it. Look at the little one," she went on, "he is fast asleep."

The word asleep made Looby think of Andy and Teddy and she thought it was time she began to go back especially as the sun had begun to set. She said goodbye to the mother deer and stroked the smooth soft fur on the little fawn's head. He was so tired that he didn't even stir.

"Thank you for helping him to walk," said the deer. "And come and see us whenever you like."

"Thank you," Looby said, "I will." She ran quickly through the trees and found the path. Everything looked so sparkling in the evening sun that she kept stopping to look at a flower or a pretty stone or a little green frog—once she saw three baby rabbits playing together and she watched them for so long that she didn't notice that there was no more sun and that it was beginning to get quite dark.

She hurried along the path until she came to a place where it divided into two and she couldn't remember which of the two she should take. In the end she took the one which seemed to go straight on but she did not come to any place she knew. It grew darker and

darker and she began to cry. "I'm lost," she said with tears running down her cheeks. "I don't know where I am and I shall never see Andy Pandy and Teddy again."

Tired and frightened she sat down on a stone and presently heard the sound of some large animal nearby. She called out "Who are you, please?"

A gruff voice said "I am Brock the Badger. Who are you and why are you making that noise?"

"I'm Looby Loo and I'm

crying because I'm lost and it's dark and I'm frightened."

"Where do you live?"

"At the little house next to the big farm, with Andy Pandy and Teddy and the White Kitten and Rags," said Looby.

"Rags?"

"He's a dog," she said, "only a little one."

"Ha!" said Brock. "I know *him*. He's run after me once or twice but he'd be very surprised if we ever came face to face. I'm three times bigger than he is."

"Oh," cried Looby, "but you wouldn't hurt him, would you?"

"Badgers don't hurt anybody," Brock said, "but I might try to teach him not to run after other animals. But what are we to do about you?" He sat near Looby Loo and went on, "I know where the farm is and I think I remember the little house."

"Oh *please*, Brock, do take me there."

"Well," said the badger. "I'll walk in front and you follow."

"But it's so dark," cried poor Looby, "that I should soon lose sight of you."

Brock said. "Then let's walk side by side. If you look down you'll see the white stripe down

the middle of my face however dark it is. Come along."

"Oh, thank you," cried Looby jumping up. "How kind you are."

The badger trotted off so quickly that she found it hard to keep up with him but she stayed close to him, stumbling over stones sometimes because she kept her eyes on that white stripe jogging along beside her.

It seemed a very long way to the edge of the wood but at last there they were at the farm gates and could see Andy Pandy's house.

"I won't come any further," said Brock. "Your dog friend might come running out and I don't want to be bothered with him just now barking and snapping at me. I have to get back home as quickly as I can."

Looby stooped down and patted the badger's head. "I shall always remember how kind you have been and I shall tell Rags all about you and say that he must never never run after you again."

The badger almost smiled. "Does he always do what you tell him?" he asked.

"Well no," said Looby, "but he will this time, when he knows how good you have been to me."

The badger said, "Run along now, Looby Loo. I'll watch until you get to your own house."

She was surprised to see that although it had been so dark in the wood it was much lighter outside. She ran off and when she reached the garden gate turned to wave to the badger. All she could see was the white stripe which turned away and disappeared. Then she crawled through the cat flap in the kitchen door and crept upstairs. Andy and Teddy were still fast asleep and never knew how their own rag doll had played with a little fawn, got lost in the wood and been rescued by a kind hearted badger with a white stripe stretching all the way from his eyes to the tip of his nose.

THE LITTLE HEDGEHOG

1 "Look what I've found in the garden," cried Teddy. "It's a little hedgehog," Andy said.

2 Teddy tried to stroke it but drew his paw away quickly. "It's nothing but prickles," he cried.

3 "Let's give it some milk," Andy said. He fetched some in a saucer.

4 The little hedgehog drank it all up then made a funny little noise as it looked round.

5 "It's looking for something," said Andy. "Perhaps it wants its mother."

6 He went into the shed and came out with a garden broom with stiff bristles.

7 He laid it down on the grass and the little hedgehog curled up against it and went to sleep.

8 Teddy laughed. "It must think it's his mother," he said—"it's just as prickly as she must be."

A PAPER CAP FOR A SMALL BOY

1 Cut a strip of paper long enough and wide enough to cover a
Little boy's head from back to front

WHAT TO USE
stiff paper
paints
scissors
basin
glue

2 Put a small basin upside-down on one end of the strip and draw a line round it

3 Cut a round end to form a peak

4 Bend the back of the peak backwards and paint it with stripes or dots

CUT A NARROW STRIP OF PAPER LONG ENOUGH TO GO ROUND A SMALL BOY'S HEAD

STICK IT ON TO THE OUTSIDE OF THE PEAK

Bend the cap
to fit the
boy's head

Stick the strip
on to the back
of the cap

Andy Pandy made one
for Teddy

THE SLEDGES

"Brrr, brrr," said Andy Pandy coming in from the garden and quickly shutting the door one day in the winter. "It's very cold outside and I wonder if we shall have some snow soon."

Teddy smiled. He loved the snow. "We can make a snowman and play snowballs, and slide and toboggan and . . ."

"So we can, Teddy," said Andy laughing. "But it's not snowing yet so we shall have to wait until it does."

Later in the evening Teddy and Andy were sitting quietly by the fire looking at picture books. After a while Andy looked at Teddy. He was sitting there with his eyes closed and with a contented little smile on his face.

"Poor Teddy," said Andy. He leaned across.

"Come along, Teddy, upstairs to bed. It's so uncomfortable to sleep sitting up."

Teddy opened his eyes. "Yes," he said and very slowly he got up and tottered off up to bed. "It was lovely on the sledge, wasn't it? I'm glad it snowed," he said sleepily.

Andy looked at him. What did he mean?

"It hasn't snowed yet," he said, but Teddy was nearly at the top of the stairs and didn't hear.

"Oh, well," said Andy. "He must have been dreaming," and then he too went up the stairs to bed.

The next morning when Andy and Teddy woke up they could feel how cold it was.

"Perhaps it's snowing now," said Teddy, and they both ran across to the window to see.

And there it was, lovely deep, white sparkling snow.

They dashed downstairs and had their breakfast very quickly and then put on their outdoor clothes.

"Wrap up very warm," said Andy. "Come on, Rags," he called. But Rags was outside as soon as the door was open, running up and down in the snow and barking loudly.

At first Andy and Teddy just ran about in the snow, then Andy scooped up a handful of snow and threw it at Teddy. Teddy threw a handful back and in no time at all snowballs were being thrown in all directions, even Rags joining in and trying to catch some in his mouth.

After a time they both felt quite hot.

"I'm going indoors for a drink of orange juice," said Andy.

"Me too," said Teddy.

"Phoo," said Teddy as he sank into a chair holding a

mug of orange juice. "How lovely," but they soon cooled down and before long were rushing about in the snow again.

Then Andy went round to the garden shed. Teddy followed him.

"What have you come to fetch?" asked Teddy as Andy opened the door. He watched while Andy went into a corner behind some boxes and brought out a sledge.

"Come along, Teddy, we're going to the big hill. Rags, Rags," he called, and Rags came running over to them. So with Andy dragging the sledge and Rags rushing up and down beside them they made their way down the lane. As they passed the gate leading to the duck's pond they looked over the top.

"Oh, poor things," said Andy Pandy, "the pond is frozen over and the ducks are standing round the edge waiting for the ice to be broken so that they can have somewhere to swim. Come along, let's go and help them."

So Andy and Teddy opened the gate and went into the yard. "Quack, quack, quack," said the ducks waddling up to them.

"Wuff, wuff, wuff," barked Rags wagging his tail.

"Quiet, Rags," said Teddy. "Don't frighten them."

"Perhaps he was only telling them that we've come to help," said Andy stroking Rags' head.

He looked around for a heavy stick and when he reached the edge of the pond he started to chip at the ice which was thinner at the side. He made

a little hole and gradually chipped and chipped until he had made a hole big enough for the ducks to get into and move about in the water. They swam about saying, "Quack, quack, quack."

"I expect they're saying, thank you, now," whispered Teddy to Andy.

They went back out of the gate and then across the field towards the hill. At the top of the big hill, Andy looked for the best place. It should be a gentle slope, very smooth with no bumps or bushes to run into. When he had found the right one he said. "I'll sit in front to guide the sledge and you get up very close behind me and hold on tight." He sat on the front of the sledge and took the cords in his hands.

Teddy got on behind, squeezing up very close.

"There's not much room," he said.

Suddenly the sledge moved forward, away they went down the hill, faster and faster and faster to the bottom.

"That was lovely, wasn't it?" said Andy. And getting off, he turned round to pull the sledge up the hill again.

There was no answer from Teddy. He wasn't there!

"Teddy, where are you?" called Andy, and looking up he saw a little bundle of fur in the snow halfway up the slope.

"Teddy," he shouted. "What happened?"

"I fell off," said Teddy laughing. "There wasn't enough room for me. I'm too fat."

"Perhaps you've been eating too many sticky buns," said Andy smiling. "Well, if we can't sledge together, we shall have to go one at a time, although it won't be nearly so much fun. As I've just been almost by myself, you can go the next time."

So Teddy took his turn and with a gentle push from Andy he was soon rushing away to the bottom of the slope. But

surprised to see Rags go running along behind the sledge. Suddenly he slipped on an icy patch and fell over and rolled over and over so fast that he went right past Andy on the sledge.

"I'm cold again now," said Teddy taking the sledge from Andy who had puffed his way up to the top again.

So it was Teddy's turn once again and Andy had to wait.

While he was rushing down suddenly Teddy had an idea.

"I shan't be long," he called to Andy. He jumped off the sledge and dashed off back through the field towards their house.

"I wonder why he's doing that?" said Andy to himself.

He kept looking in the direction which Teddy had taken and after a while he saw Teddy come tramping back through the snow.

"Whatever has he brought with him?" thought Andy.

When Teddy got closer Andy could see that he had a round metal tea-tray under his arm and Rags' lead wrapped round one of his paws.

"What are you going to do?" Andy Pandy asked.

Teddy just smiled and walked

then he had to drag the sledge all the way back up to the top of the hill again.

Teddy puffed and panted as he gave the sledge to Andy.

"It takes longer to bring it back up than to go down," he panted. "And now I'm so hot."

"You can cool down when I'm having my turn," said Andy laughing.

Andy sped down the slope on the sledge again and Teddy was

past Andy and still carrying the tea-tray went to the top of the slope. He put the tray down on the snowy slope and then he sat on it. He gave himself a little push off with his paws and then he was off down the slope with Rags slipping and sliding along after him.

Andy climbed on the sledge and followed him down the hill.

But when they turned to go up the hill again Teddy put

his tray on the sledge and said, "Rags, Rags. Come here, good dog. We want you."

Suddenly Andy Pandy guessed what Teddy was going to do and he burst out laughing. "Give me the lead," he said.

Teddy laughed too and the two of them fastened Rags' lead on to the cords of the sledge, and away he went dragging the sledge and the tray up the hill so easily that neither Andy nor Teddy could keep up with him.

"Wasn't it a good idea?" said Teddy, as they panted up the hill.

"It was a splendid idea, Teddy," said Andy. "But what made you think of the tea-tray?"

Teddy smiled. "Well," he said, "last night when I went to sleep by the fire, I had a lovely dream. It was all snowy and we were out with our sledges and the one that I had was round like a tray and that was what made me think of it."

"Well," said Andy. "I think you are a very clever little bear."

They stayed on the slope with their sledges for a long time. Then Andy looked up at the sky. It was getting quite dark.

"I think we should go home now," he said. "It's getting dark. Besides I'm getting very tired, too. Are you tired, Teddy?"

Teddy nodded. "And hungry too," he said.

Andy laughed. Teddy was always hungry.

When they got home Andy put the sledge away in the shed and Teddy put the tray under the sink. Rags had a whole sausage for his supper because he had pulled the sledge so well and when they had all gone to bed Looby Loo got up and wiped the tray which was wet because Teddy had put it away with a lot of snow on it.

RAGS ON A LEAD

1 Rags likes going for walks but sometimes he runs away and won't come back when Andy calls him.

2 One day when Andy Pandy had caught him he said, "Next time you go out you'll have to be on a lead."

3 The next day Rags pretended he didn't want to go out. Andy put the lead on but Rags just sat down and wouldn't move.

4 Suddenly Rags had an idea. He raced off pulling Andy Pandy behind him.

5 Teddy ran after them to see what was going to happen and so did the White Kitten.

6 Rags raced towards a big tree and ran round and round it.

7 And there they were with the lead wrapped round the tree and Andy pulling one way and Rags the other.

8 "Undo his lead, Teddy," Andy shouted. "He's more trouble on a lead than without one."

9 Andy had just begun to unwind the lead when the White Kitten took the other end in his mouth.

10 As soon as it was unwound, he ran up the tree with it.

11 Andy Pandy had to climb the tree and go after him.

12 But the White Kitten climbed higher and higher.

13 Andy couldn't get the lead away from the White Kitten until they were at the very top of the tree.

14 Then he threw it down and cried, "Catch, Teddy."

15 But it wasn't Teddy who caught it. It was Rags.

16 He ran away with it and hid it under the blanket in his basket.

17 When Andy and Teddy came in they looked everywhere for it but couldn't find it.

18 Because naughty Rags was sitting on it.

A PICTURE TO PAINT

THE SACK RACE

1 "I'm tired of all my toys," Teddy said one day. "I want something new to play with."

2 "Let's find something in the shed," Andy said. But there was nothing but garden tools and some old sacks.

3 "We could have a sack race," Andy said. He put both his legs in one and held it up with his hands.

4 Then Teddy did the same and they both jumped out of the shed into the garden.

5 "Now," said Andy, "let's race from here to the willow tree." He started off but almost at once Teddy fell over.

6 Soon he was far behind. Andy was sure of winning the race until Teddy passed him.

7 But look what that bad little bear had done. He had a sack on each leg so of course he could run faster.

8 But Andy took one very big leap and just got to the willow tree first.

SARDINES FOR TEA

Andy and Teddy
Had sardines for tea,
With brown bread and butter
And buns, as you see.

White Kitten came sniffing
And looked at the dish.
"Miaow," he said softly,
"You know I like fish."

At first no one took
Any notice, so he
Cried louder and louder,
"SARDINES FOR ME."

"You're a bad little cat
To come worrying us,
But I'll give you a fish
If you don't make a fuss."

"So here's a sardine,
Please take it away
Go out in the garden,
Now do as I say."

The Kitten said, "Thanks,"
And went off with a smile
And when he had gone
There was peace for a while.

Then a noise in the garden
Made Andy look round,
He saw the White Kitten
Come in with a bound.

A stream of small kittens
Poured in through the door.
They miaowed and they purred.
Then they sat on the floor.

"They're my friends," said White Kitten,
"They have come here to tea.
May they each have a fish
Like the one you gave me?"

"Oh, Teddy," cried Andy
"This is a surprise.
Their mouths are all open
And *look* at their eyes."

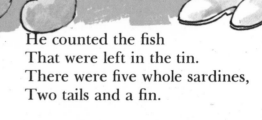

He counted the fish
That were left in the tin.
There were five whole sardines,
Two tails and a fin.

There isn't much over,
I wish we had more.
But we'll put what we have
Down here on the floor.

The kittens were mewing
And raising their paws
And one specially small one
Was showing his claws.

"There's one on my plate,"
Teddy said with a smile.
"That ought to keep them
Quiet for a while."

"I have one too,"
Andy Pandy then said,
And soon all the kittens
Were happily fed.

When they had finished
There wasn't a peep,
Or a mew or a cry.
They had all gone to sleep.

FILL IN THE SQUARES
TO FINISH THE PICTURE

THE BAD BILLY-GOAT

At the end of Andy Pandy's garden there is a big field. It belongs to a farm and the farmer lets Andy and Teddy go and play in it. An-loo-tee, whose name is a mixture of part of Andy's name, part of Looby Loo's and the "Tee" at the end stands for Teddy, is a little friendly donkey who lets them ride on his back. They are all very fond of him.

Sometimes a billy-goat is in the field. Teddy is a little afraid of him because he once ran after him and butted him with his horns. Teddy flew up into the air and fell down into the soft grass. He wasn't hurt, only rather surprised and when he sat up he was sure he saw Billy laughing at him. But one day when they went into the field to take the donkey some apples, there was the billy-goat harnessed to a very smart little cart painted red and with yellow wheels.

They didn't see the farmer but they heard a voice from

the other side of the hedge which said that they could ride round the field in the cart if they liked. The billy-goat stood there looking as good as gold and as quiet as a lamb.

"I don't think I want to go in the cart," Teddy said. "The billy-goat might run away."

"Let's try him first," Andy Pandy said. "We'll put Looby Loo in the cart and if he goes quietly, we'll get in after. He can't hurt Looby because she's only a rag doll."

Andy didn't know that when he and Teddy were asleep, or away, or just not looking, Looby could run about and play as well as they could, but when she was with them, she was what he said she was, just a floppy rag doll.

"I know what we'll do," Andy said. "We will both ride on An-loo-tee and walk beside the

goat cart." He put Looby in the cart and tied her in, just in case the goat went too fast for he didn't want her to fall out even if she was only a rag doll.

The billy-goat stood quietly while Andy was busy with Looby Loo and he watched while Andy climbed up on to An-loo-tee's back and gave Teddy a hand to help him climb up behind him.

Then he said, "Gee-up, An-loo-tee — gee-up, Billy."

And sure enough, An-loo-tee trotted along and the billy-goat trotted along beside him. They went all round the field and Looby Loo smiled to herself and really enjoyed it. When they had come back to where they had started Andy Pandy

said, "Look how quiet and good Billy is. Let us have a ride in the cart now."

As soon as Billy heard that, he dashed off at full speed across the field and, without waiting to be told, An-loo-tee galloped after him with Andy and Teddy clinging on to him as hard as they could. Andy shouted, "Stop Billy, stop, stop." But Billy took no notice —round and round he went, this way and that way while poor Looby Loo was tossed from side to side and was very glad that Andy Pandy had tied her in.

Now all this time, Rags and the White Kitten were playing in Andy's garden but when they heard all the shouting they ran to the gate to see what was going on. The White Kitten climbed a tree, he always felt safe if he was high up but Rags

jumped over the gate and barking joyfully he joined in the chase. So there was Looby tearing along in the goat cart, and the donkey galloping along behind and Andy and Teddy both shouting and now Rags running beside Billy and snapping at his heels.

Suddenly Billy turned and running faster than ever went straight for the hedge and jumped right over it, cart, Looby and all. But just before, guessing what he was going to do, Rags jumped into the cart so he went over the hedge too. An-loo-tee pulled up at the hedge—he didn't jump over, he stood still while Andy and Teddy saw Billy and Looby and Rags racing down the lane as hard as they could go.

"Whatever shall we do?" Andy cried. "We'll never catch them."

An-loo-tee said, "Hee haw, hee haw" and he looked round at Andy and Teddy as if to say, "Leave it to me. I'll catch them." Then he trotted off to the farm gate and stood there, then he nudged it with his nose but he couldn't open it. So Andy Pandy slipped down off his back and opened it, and shut it again after An-loo-tee had trotted through.

There was no one about in the farm yard but a few hens because everyone was busy working in the fields, so the little donkey went over to a shed where a splendid big horse, named Dobbin, was enjoying a bundle of hay the farmer had put there for him. As soon as he saw An-loo-tee he left the hay and came out into the farmyard—it seemed as if he knew that the donkey wanted to tell him something.

They did seem to be talking. They rubbed their noses together and made little soft sounds until something An-loo-tee said made Dobbin suddenly lift up his head and neigh, not once or twice, but over and over again just as if he couldn't stop laughing.

Andy Pandy looked anxiously up at him, not knowing quite what to do and feeling really worried about Looby Loo and

Rags and Dobbin gave one or two snorts and pushed Andy gently towards An-loo-tee as if to say "get on again". So Andy climbed on to the little donkey's back and sat once more in front of Teddy. Then they all set off at a good trot out into the lane but instead of going the way Billy goat went, they turned the other way.

Side by side, the splendid big horse and the little donkey with Andy Pandy and Teddy on his back went steadily on until they came to a little path so narrow that the hedges on either side almost touched them. Andy noticed that there were other paths branching off and that Dobbin who was leading, always took the right hand turn and suddenly he knew what they were going to do. They were going to make a big circle and come out on to the lane much further up than Billy could have gone in the time and then turn to meet him.

Now you might think that Billy would have gone much faster than Dobbin or An-loo-tee but when a goat cart has been made to jump over a hedge it doesn't go quite as well as it did. One of the wheels wobbled a bit and the

brake had got jammed so that however hard Billy pulled he couldn't get along very quickly. He was bothered by Rags too because he kept up a whole stream of different kinds of barks, squeals, growls, loud barks, yapping barks and every now and then a sort of roaring noise like a lion.

So Billy stopped so suddenly that Rags was shot out of the cart into the lane. He was just going to jump in again when he saw in the distance,

a horse and a donkey, and two little figures he knew very well. He raced towards them, his ears flapping, his tail wagging and with happy barks. When he met them he turned and all five, Andy Pandy, Teddy, An-loo-tee, Dobbin and Rags went towards Billy and the goat cart.

When they came up to him, they spread out and filled up the lane so that no one could pass and then they stopped. Andy got off the donkey's back and went to untie poor Looby Loo who had been so shaken about that she had lost both hair ribbons, one shoe had come off and could never be found and there was a great tear in her sleeve where it had caught in the hedge as the cart had swayed from side to side. Andy hugged her and gave her to Teddy to hold while he climbed back on to An-loo-tee.

For a few minutes Billy stared at them all but he didn't move. Then Dobbin, who was very big and strong and splendid, seized Billy's reins in his mouth, turned him round and marched him back up the lane to the farm and Billy didn't like it very much because he was rather tired after all

his racing about and pulling the cart and Dobbin trotted off so smartly that he could hardly keep up.

When they reached the farm Andy Pandy told the farmer what had happened and that he was very sorry that the pretty little cart didn't look so shiny-new as it had, but the farmer said that he could soon put that right and that the goat

had been very naughty but that sometimes goats were. Then Andy said that perhaps Rags had been naughty too because he had snapped at Billy's heels and Rags let his ears hang down almost to the ground and there wasn't the slightest sign of a wag in his tail.

But the farmer said, "Oh, well, dogs will be dogs. Don't worry any more, no one was hurt and I daresay Andy Pandy will be able to find some new ribbons for Looby Loo." Then he pushed his cap back and scratched his head. "What beats me," he added, "is how Dobbin managed to get out."

An-loo-tee and Dobbin looked at each other and they both turned their heads so that the farmer should not see that they were trying not to laugh.

A PAPER HAT FOR A LITTLE GIRL

WHAT TO USE
stiff paper
paints
scissors
basin
glue

3 Cut it out

4 Paint a pattern on it

1 Turn a big basin upside-down

2 Put it on the paper and draw a
line round it

5 Fold it in half to make a crease
along the middle

CUT A STRIP OF PAPER LONG ENOUGH TO GO UNDER A LITTLE GIRL'S CHIN

Stick one end of the strip on the top edge of the hat

Stick the other end on to the other side of the hat

Andy Pandy made one

for little Looby Loo

TWO LITTLE CHICKS

1 One day Teddy found two eggs in the hedge at the end of the garden.

2 "Look Andy," he cried. "Eggs for tea."

3 He put them on the table. "I wonder what that tapping noise is," Andy said, and went to see.

4 The tapping came from the eggs. Do you see why? First one, then two, little chicks popped out of the eggs.

5 They began to run about the kitchen table. Andy and Teddy could hardly believe their eyes.

6 "Catch them," cried Andy. "We must take them straight back to their mother."

7 Teddy fetched a basket and they popped them in. "Quick," said Andy. "Let's run with them to the hen-house."

8 "No," said Teddy. "The hedge. That's where their mother lives."

Here are Andy, Teddy and Looby Loo at the seaside. Teddy is trying to count all the seagulls hidden in the picture. Can you show him where they are? There are eight in all.